Books should be returned or renewed by the
last date stamped above

RODDA (EMILY)

Bob and the House

Elves.

D0255742

Bob
and the
House Elves

EMILY RODDA

illustrated by

Tim Archbold

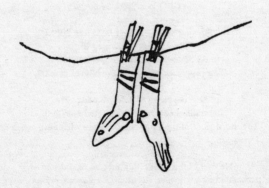

BLOOMSBURY
CHILDREN'S
BOOKS

First published in Australia in 1998
Australian Broadcasting Corporation,
GPO Box 9994, Sydney

First published in Great Britain in 2001
Bloomsbury Publishing Plc,
38 Soho Square, London, W1D 3HB
This paperback edition first published in 2002

A CIP catalogue record of this book is available from the British Library
ISBN 0 7475 5529 X

Printed in Great Britain by Clays Ltd, St Ives plc

10 9 8 7 6 5 4 3 2

For my own Bob the Builder,
with love – ER

For Rosie and John – TA

Chapter 1

Bob the Builder was a very happy man. He lived alone in a little messy house that suited him just fine. He looked after himself quite well. He swept the floor on the first of the month, and made his bed on Sundays. He always meant to clean the bath, but it never seemed to need it. Most nights he ate baked beans out of a tin, and watched TV. On Saturday mornings he did his shopping. On Saturday nights his mates came round for a game of cards, and they all ordered take-away pizza.

One Thursday morning, Bob woke up and went downstairs as usual. He knew at once that something was wrong. Someone had cleaned his kitchen. Nothing looked the same. Even the kettle. Someone had washed the windows. He could see straight through. He could see his garden, and the sun, and his new neighbour, Lily Sweet, hanging out her clothes. And on the table, instead of the Cornflakes box, was a dainty plate of fairy bread and a flower in a vase.

'What's this?' said Bob, amazed. He sat down at the table, and ate some fairy bread to settle his nerves. And then he got an awful fright. Three tiny creatures skittered from behind the fridge. Next minute, they were holding hands, and dancing in a ring.

'Crikey!' said Bob. 'So that's it! I got elves!'

He scratched his bristly chin. 'Scat!' he roared, and waved his arms.

The elves giggled. It was a twittering, twinkling sound that sent shivers up Bob's spine. He rolled up his paper and whacked!

But he missed.

Chapter 2

The next day, when Bob woke up, his hair was a mass of fairy knots. The whole house was horribly clean and bright. There were flower petals in the bath, and fairy dust in the Cornflakes. And elves were everywhere.

'Crikey, this is awful!' groaned Bob.

But things got worse and worse.

The elves had cleaned his working boots. They'd washed his blue singlet, mended his shorts, and polished his hard hat. He had to go to work all clean. His mates just laughed and laughed.

There was a fairy cake in his lunch box, and fairy bread as well. He had to eat them. He was hungry. His mates laughed even more.

Bob stomped into his house that night determined to clean out all the elves.

But while he'd been away, things had got out of hand.

'Crikey! It's a plague,' he said.

Tomorrow night, his mates were coming round for cards. He had to get rid of the elves by then. But how?

He tried loud music.

He tried throwing things.

He set traps.

He stood and shouted at the top of his voice.

But nothing worked.

Bob knew he needed help. He ate some fairy bread to settle his nerves. And then he had a bright idea.

'I can't be the only bloke with elves,' he said. 'There must be some sort of cure.'

Chapter 3

On Saturday morning, Bob went to the chemist shop. It was crowded.

'Can I help you, sir?' said a lady in a pale pink smock.

Bob went red. He felt embarrassed to admit his problem. But he knew he had to do it.

He leant across the counter. 'I got a bit of an elf problem,' he said, in a low, low voice.

'What sort of health problem do you have?' asked the lady in the pale pink smock. 'Come on, don't be shy.'

'Not health. Elf,' said Bob, going even redder. 'I got elves, at home.'

'Oh *elves*,' said the lady in the pale pink smock, standing back and looking down her nose. She turned and shouted to her friend along the counter. 'Hey, Leanne! This man's got elves. We got anything for that?'

The other customers looked at Bob. They said 'tut-tut' and edged away, or shook their heads, and smiled.

'You sure it's elves?' Leanne yelled back. 'Not pixies, are they? Gnomes, or sprites? Not fairies, dwarves or leprechauns?'

'He said elves,' bellowed the lady in the pale pink smock.

Bob wished that he could disappear. 'Crikey,' he muttered. 'Give me a break!'

'I'm sorry, sir, we're out of "Elf-Rid" at the moment,' called Leanne. 'There'll be more in on Tuesday.'

'Tuesday's much too late,' groaned Bob, and crept away.

Chapter 4

At home, Bob ate some fairy bread to settle his nerves. Then he had a bright idea. He looked up Pest Exterminators in the phone book and started ringing up. Most of the numbers didn't answer, but finally one did.

'Pesky Pest Control. Name your poison,' said a cheerful man. It was a relief to hear a friendly voice.

'Will you do a job on elves?' Bob said, in a low, low voice.

'Of course we'd do the job ourselves. Who else? There's only me and my brother here. What's biting you, mate?' Mr Pesky replied.

Bob felt himself go red again. 'Not selves. Elves,' he said. 'Me house is crawling with elves. I'm desperate.'

'Oh, *elves*,' exclaimed Mr Pesky. 'Right, then, I'm your man. You're sure it's elves you've got? Not pixies, maybe? Gnomes, or sprites? Not fairies, dwarves or leprechauns?'

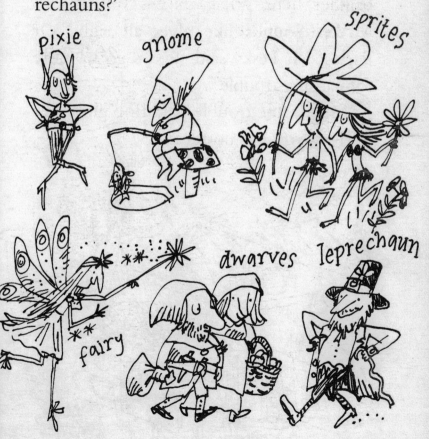

pixie

gnome

sprites

fairy

dwarves

leprechaun

'Crikey, I don't know,' cried Bob. 'What's the difference?'

'Oh, there's all the difference in the world, mate,' Mr Pesky said.

Bob thought a bit. 'Well, mine are little, they've got small wings, they dance around a lot and they like to clean up stuff.'

'Yep. Sounds like elves all right. Or fairies,' Mr Pesky said. 'Pixies go in more for causing trouble.'

'Mine cause trouble,' said Bob gloomily. 'Crikey, you got no idea.'

Mr Pesky sighed. 'Might be a new breed, mate,' he said. I'd better come and take a look. I can fit you in Wednesday week.'

'Next Wednesday week?' roared Bob. 'I can't wait that long. I'm going bonkers! Can't you come today?'

'No way,' said Mr Pesky. 'I'm up to my eyeballs here, mate. Booked up solid. It's Wednesday week or nothing.'

'Make it nothing, then!' growled Bob. 'Mate!' He slammed down the phone. He wasn't usually so rude, but he was quite upset.

Chapter 5

Bob ate some fairy bread to settle his nerves. Then he had a bright idea.

'I know,' he said. 'I'll get a book. There's books on everything these days. There must be one to deal with this.'

So he went down to the library. He'd never been in it before. There were thousands of books all round the walls. He didn't know where to start. He knew he'd have to ask.

Behind the counter was a lady in a bright green dress. She turned around and saw him.

'Hello, Bob,' she said. 'What can I do for you?'

It was Lily Sweet, the lady who'd just moved in next door.

Bob went very, very red. He felt like running. But he knew he had to go through with this. The situation was desperate.

He leant across the counter. 'You got any books on elves?' he asked, in a low, low voice.

'Oh, yes. We have lots of books on the shelves,' Lily said. 'What sort of book did you want?'

'Not shelves, *elves*,' said Bob, going even redder. 'Have you got any books on elves?'

'Oh, *elves*,' said Lily Sweet. But she smiled, and she didn't shout. 'And is it just elves you want? Not pixies, or sprites, for example? Not fairies or gnomes or leprechauns?'

'I don't think so,' said Bob. 'I think it's elves, all right. Unless it's fairies. Or pixies. Could be a new breed, I reckon.'

Lily smiled. She had kind grey eyes. 'Let's see what we can find,' she said. She went away for a moment, and came back with a big thick book. It had a brightly coloured picture of elves, fairies and pixies on the front.

She stamped the card at the back and gave the book to Bob. 'You can keep it till next week,' she said.

'Next week will be too late,' said Bob. 'I've only got till seven tonight.'

He thanked Lily, left the library and crept off home, trying to hide the book under his coat. It was the most embarrassing walk of his life.

Chapter 6

When Bob got home, the elves were worse. He ate some fairy bread to settle his nerves. Then he had a bright idea. He pitched his tent in the living room and zipped himself inside. Then he read the book in peace, all afternoon.

At five past six he yelled '*Bingo!*' He'd found what he was looking for. There it was, in black and white, on page 117.

A Recipe Guaranteed to Banish Elves from Houses, Boats and Caravans

Tomato sauce
A cube of ice
A slice of mouldy cheese
3 snips of dirty fingernail
And 22 baked beans

Stir it well and heat it up
Then give the pan a whack.
And say these words
While turning round
With your head inside a sack:
'Elven folk!
I have spoke!
Begone, and don't come back!'

'Sounds simple enough,' said Bob.

He rushed into the kitchen with the book. He got a saucepan ready. He started to assemble the ingredients. Tomato sauce, ice, mouldy cheese, dirty fingernails – no problem. But when it came to baked beans . . .

'Crikey!' howled Bob. 'I'm all out.'

He'd been so upset that he'd forgotten to do his Saturday morning shopping.

He grabbed his wallet and ran outside. But when he got to the corner shop, it was shut.

'Open up!' he yelled, and beat on the door with his fists. But there was no one there. Tony, who owned the shop, had left long ago. After all, it was Saturday night, and he was going to the movies with his girlfriend.

Bob trailed home in despair. 'Twenty-two baked beans,' he muttered, as he walked. 'That's all I wanted. A few miserable baked beans. Was that too much to ask?'

Back in his house, Bob ate some fairy bread to settle his nerves.

And then he thought of his neighbour, Lily Sweet. Did ladies like her ever eat baked beans? he wondered.

It was worth a try.

Chapter 7

Bob went next door and knocked. Lily answered the door. When she saw him, she smiled.

'Well, hello, Bob,' she said. 'What can I do for you?'

Bob went red. 'I was just wondering,' he mumbled, 'if you'd have any baked beans at all?'

'Oh, dear. I'm very sorry, but I don't,' said Lily Sweet. 'I ate the very last of mine for dinner, just now. If only you'd come in two minutes earlier . . .'

'Oh, no!' groaned Bob, and clutched his head.

'Do you need baked beans especially?' she asked. 'I have kidney beans. I have haricot beans, and broad beans and butter beans. I have green beans, string beans, jumping beans and jelly beans. Would any of those do instead?'

'I don't reckon they would,' said Bob. 'It's a recipe, see. Tomato sauce, a cube of ice, a slice of mouldy cheese, three bits of dirty fingernail – and twenty-two baked beans.

A strange expression appeared on Lily's face. 'But — isn't that the recipe for getting rid of elves?' she asked. 'From houses, boats and caravans?'

Bob went even redder, and hung his head. 'Yeah,' he confessed. 'It was in that book I got from the library.'

Lily clasped her hands. 'So — do you have elves, Bob? In your house? Now?'

Bob knew he couldn't lie to Lily. She had such nice, kind grey eyes.

'Yeah,' he muttered. 'A whole mob of 'em. They've been driving me bonkers.

And I can't get rid of 'em, Lily. Crikey, I've tried everything.'

He looked up, to see how she was taking it. She looked very, very shocked. 'Oh, Bob,' she breathed. 'I'm so sorry.'

Bob went the reddest he'd ever been. And he was, to tell the truth, a bit disappointed. He'd thought that Lily might have tried to make him feel better, instead of worse.

'Oh, well, I s'pose it could happen to anyone,' he said bravely. 'See you around, then. Bye.' He turned to go back to his house.

'No!' Lily cried. 'Don't go. You don't understand. Oh, Bob, this is all my fault!'

Chapter 8

'*Your* fault?' Bob said. He was astounded.

'Oh, yes,' said Lily, very upset. 'I had elves at my last house, and they must have moved with me, in my furniture. They're like that, you know. Once you've got them, they tend to stay.'

'Don't I know it!' said Bob, with feeling.

Lily shook her head. 'But I had no idea they'd spread next door, into your place,' she said. 'They must have found a hole, or something. And all this time they've been worrying you. I feel terrible.'

She looked so unhappy that Bob patted her arm. 'Don't you give it another thought, Lil,' he said, trying to sound cheerful. 'Look, how about you give me some kidney beans. I'll have a go with them.'

'Oh, Bob, if only I'd known why you wanted that book!' cried Lily. 'I could have told you — that old recipe doesn't work! Even with proper baked beans. I know. I tried it when I first got elves years and years ago while I was on holiday.'

'What!?' yelled Bob. 'Doesn't work?' He went very, very red. This time, it wasn't because he was embarrassed. It was because he was furious.

'You mean I read that book in a tent for the whole rotten afternoon for nothing?' he shouted. 'You mean whoever wrote that book's a conman? A crook?' He clenched his fists, and looked around in a rage. 'Where's he hang out? I'll soon show him what's what. The low, miserable . . .'

He wasn't usually violent, but he was quite upset.

Chapter 9

'No, no,' said Lily quickly, patting Bob's arm. 'I'm sure the recipe *used* to work, a long time ago, Bob. But elves have got used to it, that's the trouble. These days it doesn't scare them at all.'

'Is that right?' said Bob, staring.

Lily nodded. 'Actually, mine quite like the mixture. On toast,' she said. 'And they've learned the words of the curse off by heart. They've made them into a song. They often sing it to put their babies to sleep at night. It sounds quite sweet, really.'

Bob the Builder was a brave man, but he knew when he was beaten.

'Then I've had it, Lil,' he said. 'I've shot me bolt. I've come to the end of the line. I'm up the creek without a paddle. In half an hour me mates are coming round for cards. They see those elves, and I'll never live it down. Oh, well.' He straightened his shoulders. 'That's life.'

Lily looked confused. 'But – if your friends are the problem, why don't you just ask your elves to keep out of the way, for a while?' she said.

'*Ask* them?' Bob was astounded, all over again. 'Crikey, I've asked them to get out of it a million times, mate. I've shouted and yelled till I'm blue in the face!'

'But shouting won't do any good!' exclaimed Lily. 'Elves never listen when you shout. It just makes them over-excited and troublesome. You have to speak softly and politely to them. Or better still, write them a note. They love notes.'

'I'm not much of a one for writing notes,' Bob mumbled, going red all over again.

'I'll help you, then,' Lily said.

Chapter 10

So Lily and Bob went into his house, and she helped him to write the note. The note said:

Dear Elves,
Would you be so kind as to leave this house from 10 minutes to 7 this evening until 2am? I am expecting guests.
Thank you very much.
With best wishes,
Yours sincerely,
Bob (the Builder)

They put the note on the fridge, where all the elves could see it. And five minutes later there wasn't an elf in sight.

'It's like magic,' said Bob.

'It's just polite,' said Lily. 'Well, I'd better be going. Your friends will be coming any minute.'

Bob took her to the door. 'Tomorrow, could you help me write a note to tell them to go away for good?' he asked hopefully. 'The elves, I mean.'

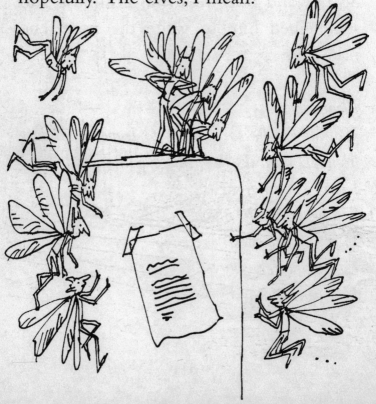

Lily looked doubtful. 'I could, I suppose. But are you sure you really want that, Bob? I know they're a bit of a nuisance sometimes, but I quite like having them around the place myself. They do all the housework for a start. They mend my clothes. And I find the fairy bread gives me bright ideas.'

Bob frowned in thought. 'Crikey, you might have a point there, Lil,' he said at last. 'I have had a few bright ideas, lately. And I'd be just as happy never to pick up a broom again, I can tell you that. Housework's a pain in the neck.'

'I agree,' said Lily. 'So what do you want to do?'

But Bob didn't quite know. Now he had another problem. He wanted the elves to go. But he wanted them to stay, as well.

Chapter 11

Bob's mates all arrived after that, so Bob and Lily couldn't talk any more. But after his mates went home, Bob thought about his problem quite a lot. He thought about it so much that he couldn't sleep.

At two a.m. the elves came back. They cleaned up all the empty glasses and pizza boxes. Then they swept the floor and washed up, and put a plate of fairy bread on the table.

Bob made himself a cup of tea, sat down at the table and ate some fairy bread to settle his nerves.

Then he had a bright idea. Without even waiting for Lily Sweet, he got paper and a pen and wrote the elves a note.

Dear Elves,

Thanks for all your work, and the fairy bread. I really appreciate it. But if you want to stay in my house, please note the following Rules:

1. Please don't clean my working boots.

2. Please don't polish my hard hat.

3. Please don't tie my hair in knots at night.

4 Please don't make the house too tidy. It makes me nervous.

5. Please note that I like Vegemite sandwiches for lunch. Or tuna sandwiches. Or cheese. Or peanut butter. Not fairy bread (or cakes).

6. Please leave the house between 7 o'clock and 2am on Saturday nights because I always have guests then.

Thank you very much.

With best wishes,

Yours sincerely,

Bob (the Builder)

Bob put the note on the fridge, and went to bed.

Chapter 12

And after that, there was no more trouble.

Now that Bob wasn't shouting at them, the elves became quiet and very easy to live with. Sometimes, they were so quiet that Bob didn't even know they were there — except that his house was always clean and tidy (but not *too* tidy), and none of his clothes had holes in them any more.

The elves obeyed all the rules Bob had written for them that night, so his mates had no more reason to laugh at him. And the Saturday card nights were always a great success. Bob's mates quite liked the house being a bit tidier. It was easier to find somewhere to sit, they said.

And of course, Bob and Lily Sweet saw a lot of one another. After all, they had plenty in common. Elves and baked beans and not liking housework, for a start.

They always had lunch together on Sundays. Sometimes they'd have it in Bob's house, sometimes in Lily's. Then they'd go for a walk in the park, while the elves cleaned up.

Bob wasn't much of a one for talking about his feelings, but after lunch one Sunday he knew the time had come. He'd worked out just what he was going to say. He ate a last piece of fairy bread to settle his nerves. Then he took Lily's hand across the table.

'Lil,' he said in a low, low voice. 'You're a special lady. No elf could take your place.'

Lily went red. 'No wealth could take your place, either, Bob,' she whispered. 'Who cares about money, anyway?'

Bob felt very, very happy. 'How about we get hitched, then?' he said.

And Lily said that was the brightest idea he'd ever had.

So they got married, and Bob made their two little houses into one big one for them to share. The elves were very pleased. The renovations made a lot of mess, so they had plenty of work to do.

And besides, being elves, there was nothing they liked better than a story with a happy ending.